THE TEARS

Written by
Luca Frigerio

Illustrated, Colored & Lettered by
Andy Licari

Designed by
Alessandra Delfino

Edited by
Bradley Golden

Bradley Golden
Founder, CEO, Editor

Marcus H Roberts
CCO, Project Manager, Submission Manager

HEY, BABY!
SKREEK

MY NAME IS NOT BABY.
PERFECT, TELL ME YOUR NAME WE SO CAN BECOME FRIENDS RIGHT AWAY!

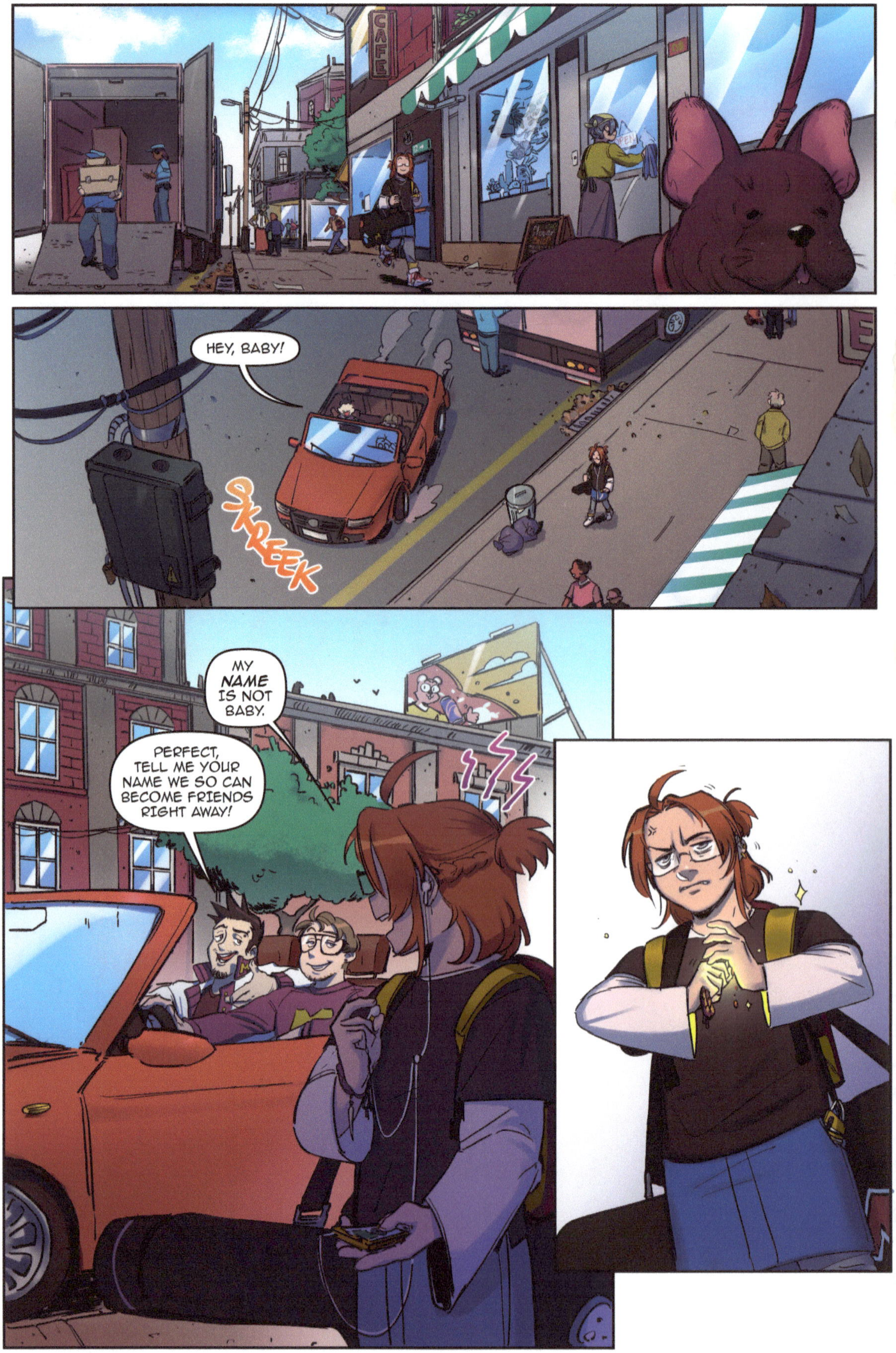

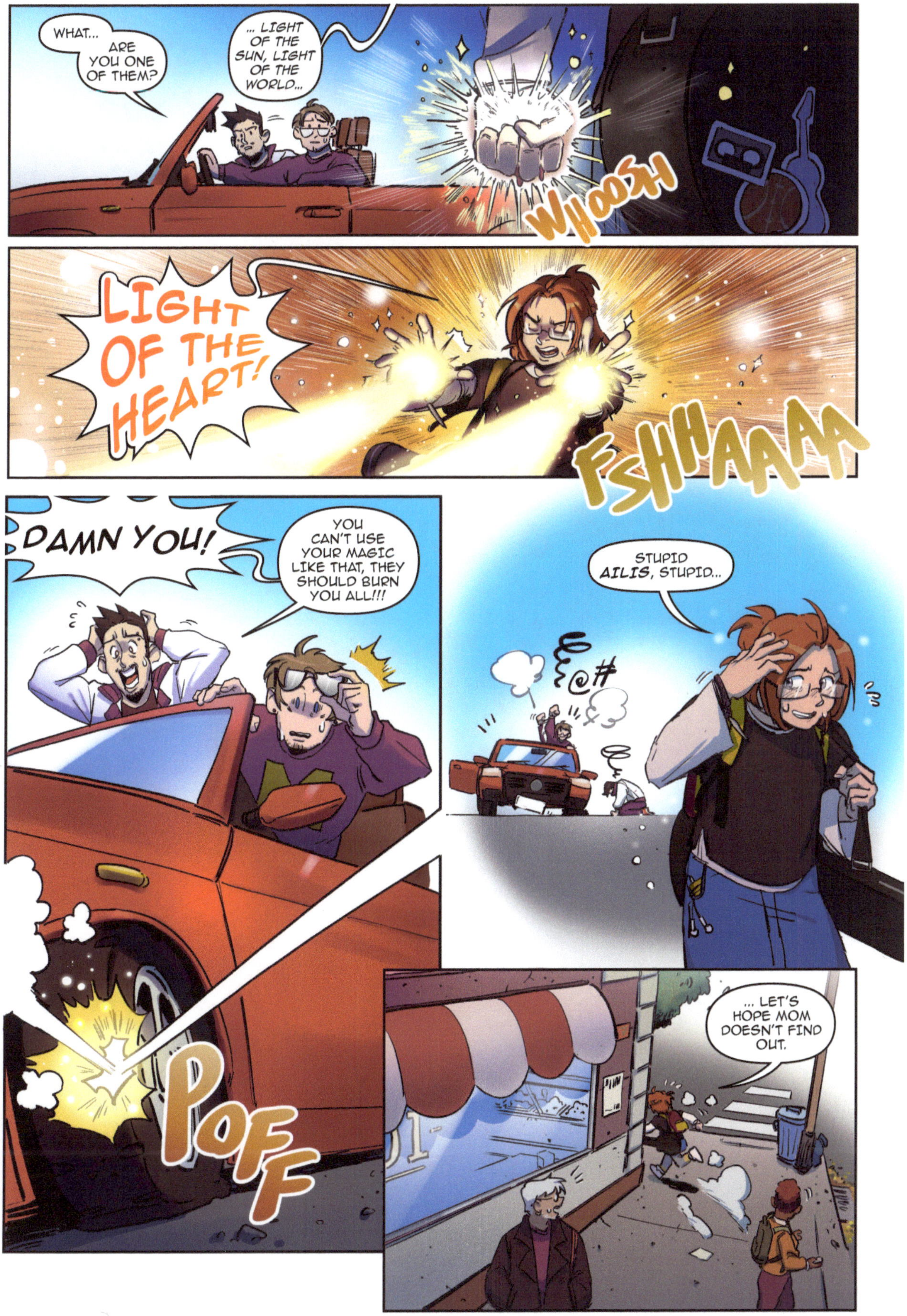

WHAT... ARE YOU ONE OF THEM?
... LIGHT OF THE SUN, LIGHT OF THE WORLD...
WHOOSH
LIGHT OF THE HEART!
FSHHAAAA
DAMN YOU!
YOU CAN'T USE YOUR MAGIC LIKE THAT, THEY SHOULD BURN YOU ALL!!!
STUPID AILIS, STUPID...
@#
POFF
... LET'S HOPE MOM DOESN'T FIND OUT.

MANNY, WHAT'S GOING ON?
WHY ARE YOU ALL OUTSIDE?
WHERE'S MY MOTHER?
AILIS... THE GUARDIANS EVACUATED US,
THEY SAY YOUR MOTHER IS A PER--
SMASH
KRAAASH
GO, RUN, AILIS!
SDENG
?
I HOPE THERE ARE NO GUARDIANS IN THE BACK.

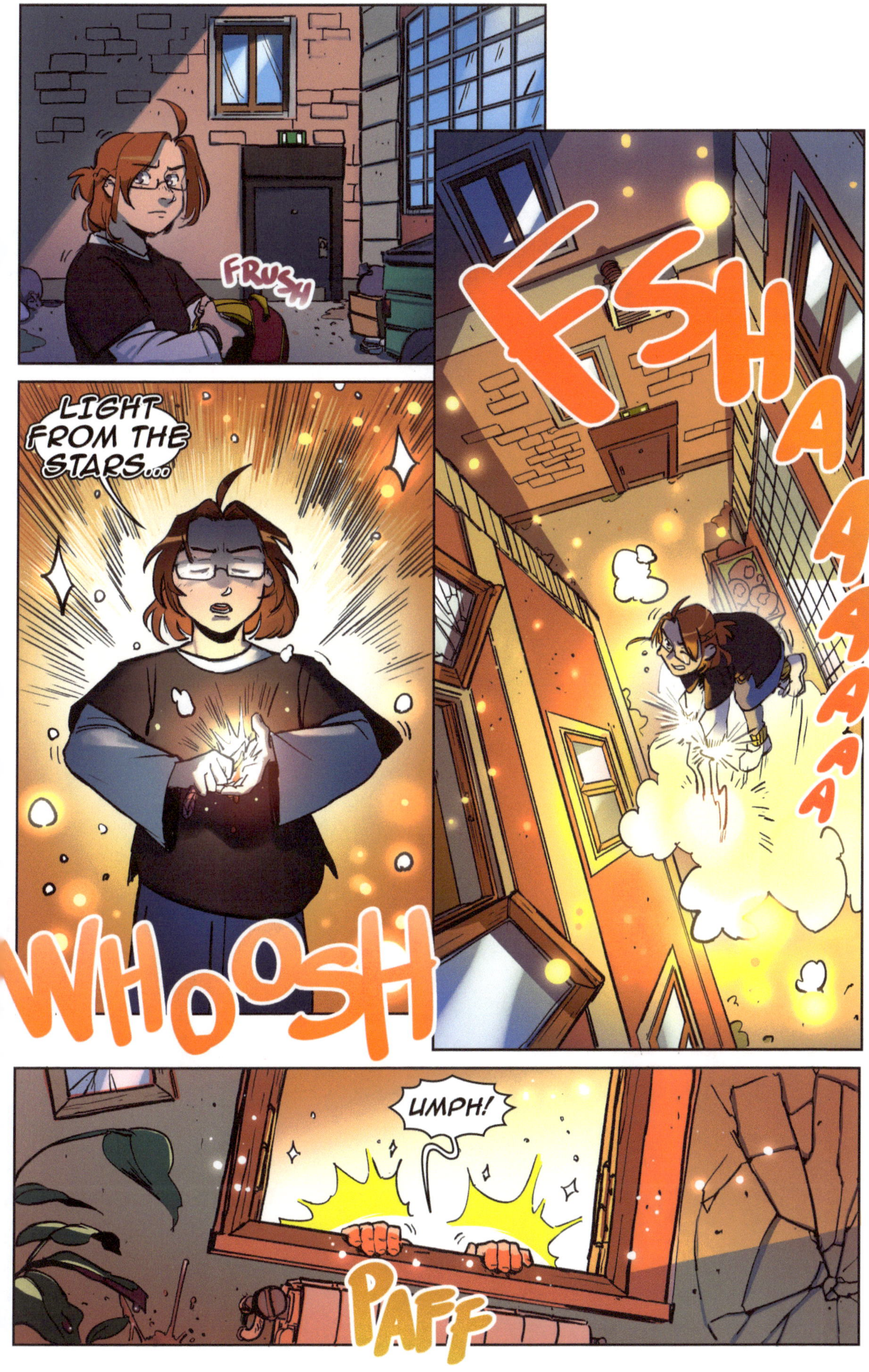

FRUSH
LIGHT FROM THE STARS...
WHOOSH
FSHAAAAAA
UMPH!
PAFF

MOM!!!
SHE IS CALLING ME,
SHE IS SUFFERING!
SHE'S CRAZY, WE HAVE TO KILL HER!
CRASH
SHE'S CALLING ME, YOU WON'T STOP ME!
STAB
MOTHER!!!

MOM? WHAT HAPPENED?
WHY ARE THE GUARDIANS HERE?
AILIS, MY BABY. I...
... SHE'S CRYING TEARS OF BLOOD, SHE IS CALLING ME...
MOM! MOM!!!
STOP AND DON'T MOVE!
CLAK

WHAT?!
LIGHT OF THE SU—
THUD

WHERE...?
OUCH, MY HEAD.

HEY!
HEY!!!

IS ANYONE THERE? WHERE AM I?
DON'T SHOUT, IT'S USELESS.

YOU'VE WOKEN UP, FINALLY.
DO YOU REMEMBER YOUR NAME?
WHAT IS THIS PLACE?
WHO ARE YOU?
I ASKED YOU IF YOU REMEMBER YOUR NAME.
SL
AM
AI-AILIS, BUT WHERE AM I?
MY MOM...

AILIS HAWKINS,
JUST ANOTHER GIRL.
EXCEPT YOU'RE A WITCH.
IT'S NOT A CRIME TO BE ONE, THE SEATTLE TREATY ALLOWS--
THAT STUPID TREATY DOESN'T DEFEND TREASON AGAINST THIS NATION.
MY MOM...
SHE'S NOT A TRAITOR.
SHE'S...
SHE IS A MURDERER AND A TRAITOR.
YOU DON'T SEEM TO KNOW ANYTHING ABOUT IT,
BUT THE FRUIT NEVER FALLS FAR FROM THE TREE.
WE SEE EVERYTHING.
EVERYTHING.

YOU KNOW WHAT TO DO.

WHAT?
WHAT???

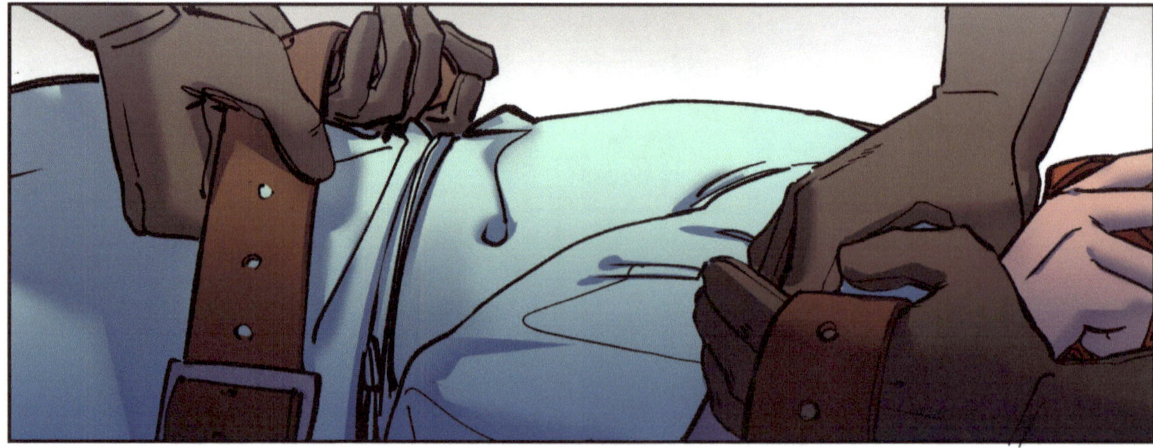

THANK YOU.
YOUR CLOTHES ARE THERE, IN THE CORNER.

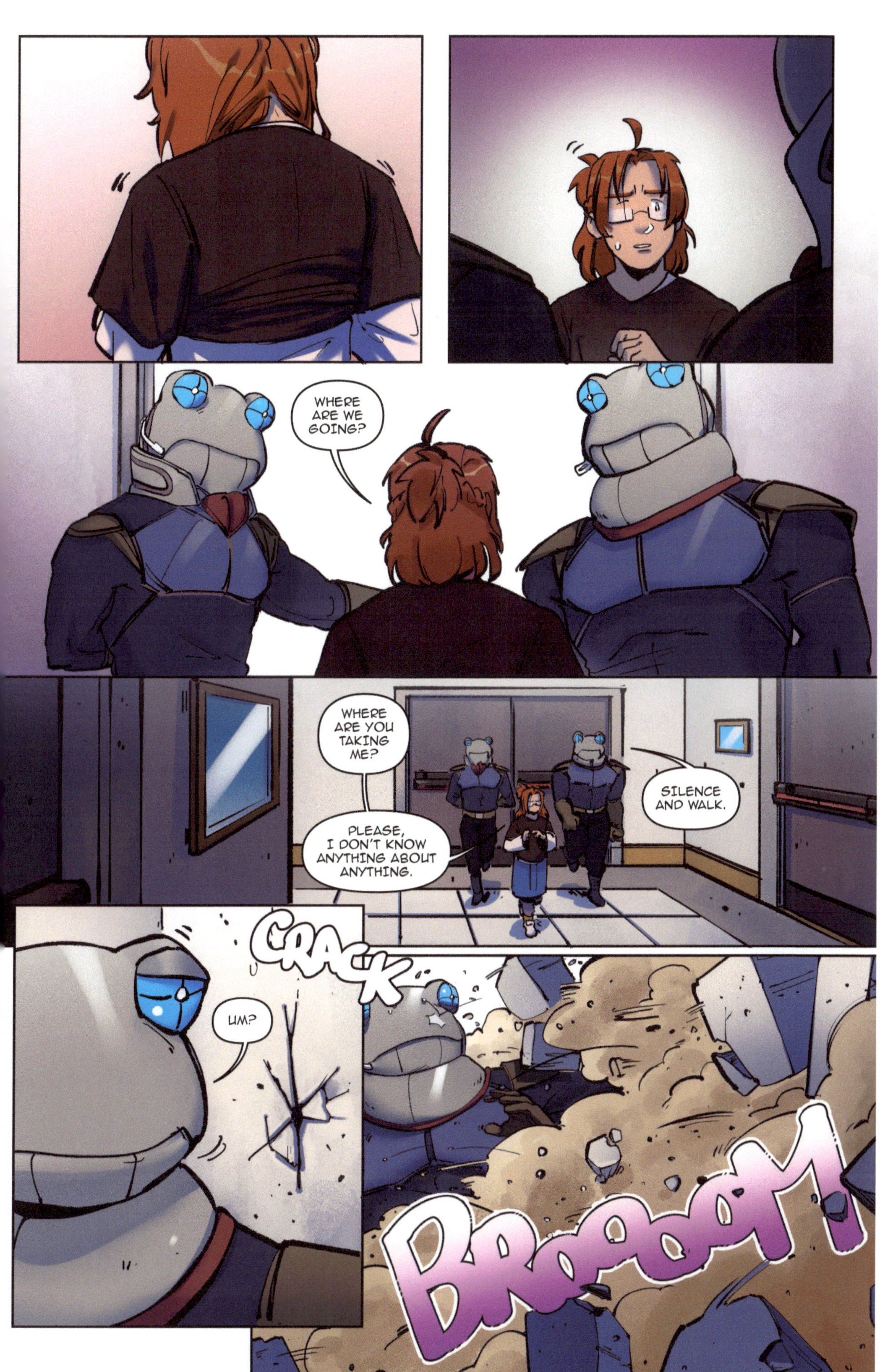

WHERE ARE WE GOING?
WHERE ARE YOU TAKING ME?
PLEASE, I DON'T KNOW ANYTHING ABOUT ANYTHING.
SILENCE AND WALK.
CRACK
UM?
BROOOM

OUCH!!!
RUMBLE
YOU!
YOU HAVE TO TELL HER.
TELL HER I DIDN'T BETRAY HER--
BANG
BANG
WHAT'S GOING ON?

LET'S TAKE HER AWAY!

I DON'T UNDERSTAND ANYTHING, WHAT'S GOING ON?
THAT WOMAN IS...
SHE'S DEAD...

NOTHING HAPPENED, IF YOU WANT TO LIVE FORGET EVERYTHING.
SHE IS DEAD.
YES, STAY QUIET NOW.
NOW GET OUT OF HERE AND DON'T MAKE ANY SUDDEN MOVES.

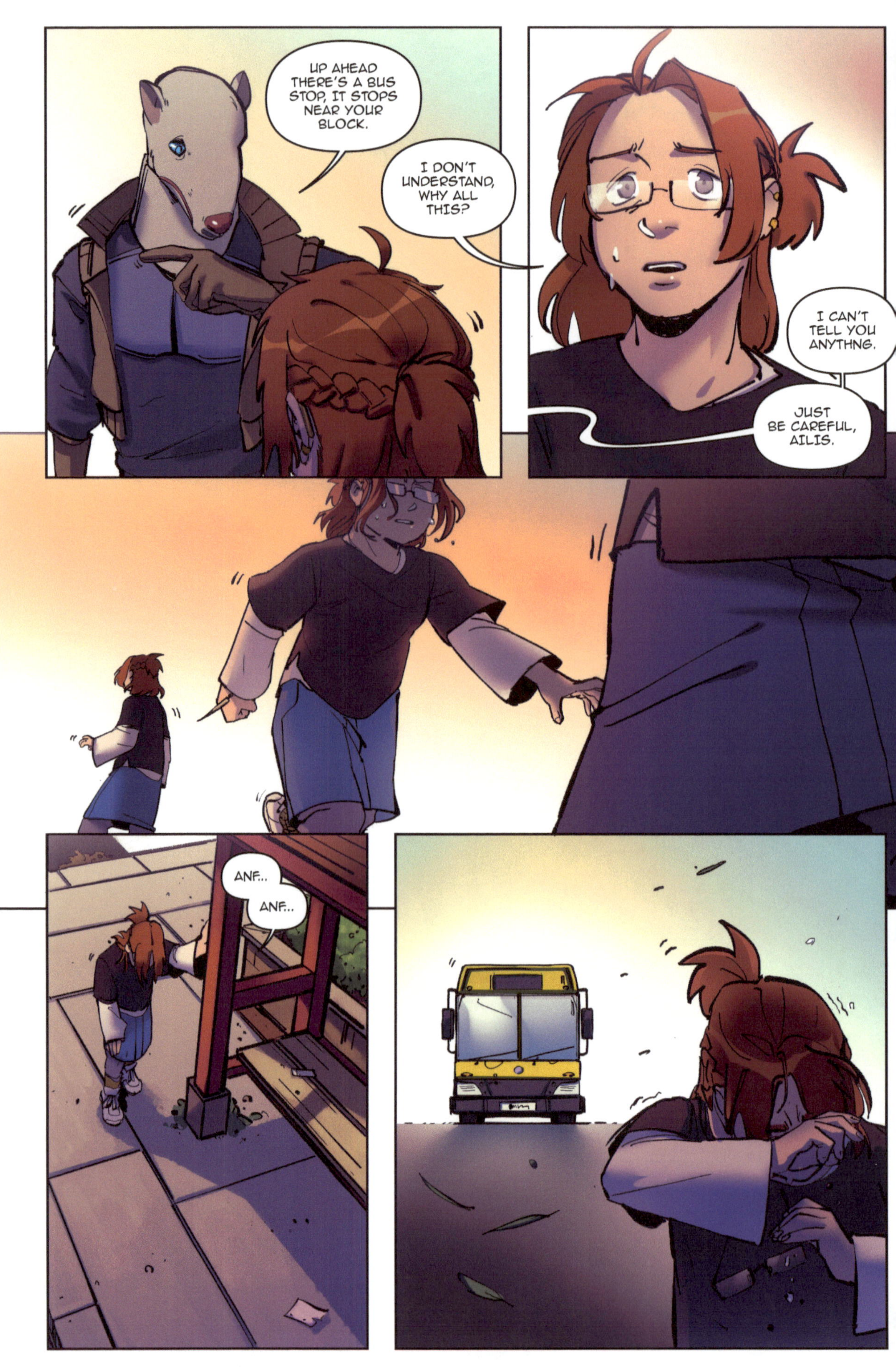

UP AHEAD THERE'S A BUS STOP, IT STOPS NEAR YOUR BLOCK.
I DON'T UNDERSTAND, WHY ALL THIS?
I CAN'T TELL YOU ANYTHNG.
JUST BE CAREFUL, AILIS.
ANF...
ANF...

IT MUST BE A NIGHTMARE, THERE'S NO OTHER WAY...
MOM...
WHERE'S MY PHONE?
I'M SURE I HAD IT.
BEFORE... BEFORE ALL THIS.

MANNY IS DEFINITELY GOING TO HELP ME.

MANNY! MANNY!!

MANNY, IT'S ME, AILIS! I NEED YOU!

MANNY CAN'T HELP YOU, IN FACT LEAVE HIM ALONE.
LEAVE US ALL ALONE!
05
BUT...

FUCK!!!

... JUST A BAD DREAM.

FUCK THE WORLD, I CAN'T TAKE IT ANYMORE.

MY ARMS...
BUT WHERE AM I?
WHO ARE YOU?

DAUGHTER OF BLOOD...
BLOOD OF THE MOTHER...

BLOOD OF THE MOTHER...
WHAT DO YOU WANT FROM ME?!
DAUGHTER OF THE BLOOD...

BLOOD CALLS FOR BLOOD...
...BLOOD CALLS FOR BLOOD.

HELP ME!

HELP ME PLEASE!!!

SOMEONE HELP ME!
WAKE UP.
AILIS, WAKE UP!

AA
AAHH
HELLO!
WHO ARE YOU?
AILIS, YOU AND I NEED TO TALK...

WHO ARE YOU? WHAT DO YOU WANT FROM ME?
I WAS ACQUAINTED TO YOUR MOTHER, WE USED TO BE...
FRIENDS.
MAISA, BY THE WINDOW.
OK!
AS I WAS SAYING, ME AND YOU NEED TO HAVE A CHAT.
NOT HERE, NOT NOW THOUGH. WE'RE NOT SAFE IN HERE.
OH REALLY? NOT SAFE?

HOLD YOUR TONGUE GIRL, I'M NOT THE ENEMY.
MAISA, WHAT'S THE SITUATION DOWN THERE?
YOU WERE RIGHT, THERE'S A BIT OF A BUSTLE.
I'M ALWAYS RIGHT, NOW LET'S LEAVE THIS PLACE BEFORE WE RUN INTO TROUBLE.
LEAVE TO WHERE?
WHY SHOULD I FOLLOW YOU?
TRUST US.

I'M SORRY, AILIS.
BUT I'M VERY SCARED.

SO FUCK YOURSELF, MANNY.
FUCK ALL OF YOU.

IT'S ALRIGHT, AILIS.
EVERYTHING WILL BE ALRIGHT.
FU--

MOVE!

FUCK!
THEY'RE HERE. RUN!
I DON'T WANT TO BE PUT IN CUFFS AGAIN!
IT WON'T HAPPEN.

STOP THERE, WITCHES.
DON'T RESIST AND NOBODY WILL GET HURT.
SOMEONE WILL GET VERY HURT INSTEAD!

LIGHT OF THE MOON, DEFEND YOUR DAUGHTERS.
RUMBLE
DEFEND THE TRUTH!
WOAH!
AGH!
GET HER!

DIE!
YOU DAMNED WITCH!

SBAM
ARE YOU DONE OR CAN WE LEAVE?
I KNOW HE WAS THERE, I HAD EVERYTHING UNDER CONTROL.
YEAH, YEAH.
YOU BEAT THEM UP ALL BY YOURSELF!
YOU'RE AMAZING!
WELL, NOT JUST BY HERSELF...
I SAID I ALREADY SAW HIM, I WOULD'VE DEFEATED HIM IN A FEW MOMENTS.
ANYWAYS THEY WERE JUST SMALL FRIES, NOT MUCH.

ARE YOU READY TO LISTEN?
I REALLY DON'T FEEL LIKE TALKING...
I SAID LISTENING, NOT TALKING.
...
YOU DON'T HAVE TO WORRY, YOU'RE SAFE WITH US!
"US"?
WHO'S "US"?
WHAT WERE YOU DOING IN MY HOUSE?

S-SORRY, I DIDN'T MEAN TO ATTACK YOU!
BUT YOU DID IT ANYWAYS, MAISA DID NOTHING WRONG.
DON'T WORRY, THAT'S JUST HOW I REACT SOMETIMES.
NOW, IF YOU'VE STOPPED ACTING LIKE A BRAT I'D LIKE TO KEEP TALKING.
OK...
I KNOW YOUR MOTHER, YOU COULD SAY WE'RE OLD FRIENDS.

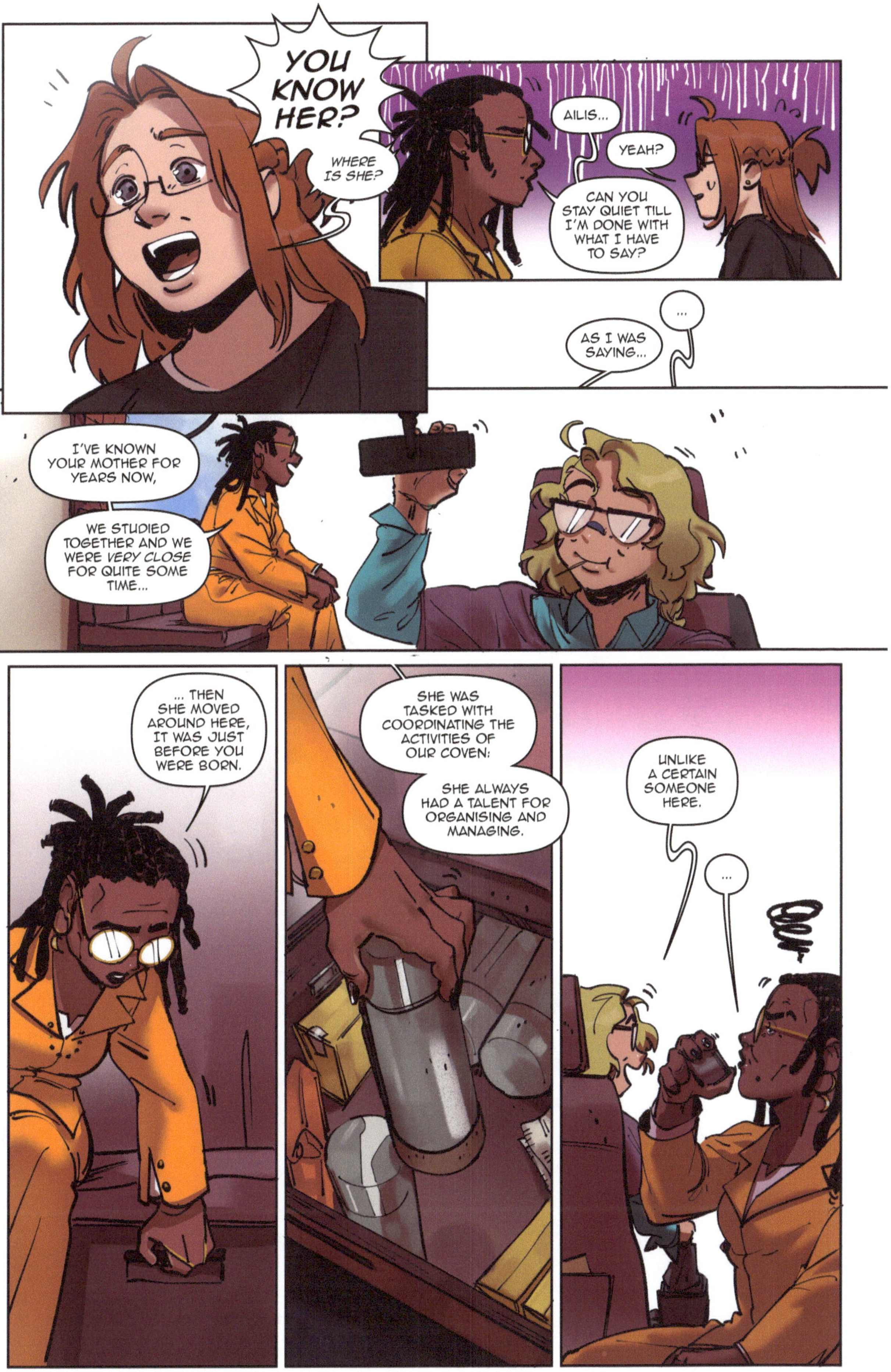

YOU KNOW HER?
WHERE IS SHE?
AILIS...
YEAH?
CAN YOU STAY QUIET TILL I'M DONE WITH WHAT I HAVE TO SAY?
...
AS I WAS SAYING...
I'VE KNOWN YOUR MOTHER FOR YEARS NOW,
WE STUDIED TOGETHER AND WE WERE VERY CLOSE FOR QUITE SOME TIME...
... THEN SHE MOVED AROUND HERE, IT WAS JUST BEFORE YOU WERE BORN.

SHE WAS TASKED WITH COORDINATING THE ACTIVITIES OF OUR COVEN:
SHE ALWAYS HAD A TALENT FOR ORGANISING AND MANAGING.

UNLIKE A CERTAIN SOMEONE HERE.
...

YEOWCH!

FOR A WHILE EVERYTHING SEEMED TO GO ACCORDING TO PLAN,

NOW YOU'RE INTERRUPTING ME?

YOU WERE BORN, THE WITCHES OF THIS AREA COULD HAVE SOMEONE THEY COULD RELY ON.

BUT...

BUT?

WHAT HAPPENED? DON'T STOP!

BUT OLIVIA, YOUR MOTHER, STARTED TO CHANGE.

SHE ACTED QUIETER, KEPT SENDING LESS AND LESS REPORTS

AND EVEN WITH ME SHE STARTED TAKING HER DISTANCES.

SHE WAS WORRIED OF BEING, HOW CAN I PUT IT, SPOTTED.

EVEN THE WITCHES FROM THIS AREA AVOIDED HAVING ALL FORM OF CONTACT WITH US...
NOTHING DRASTIC HAPPENED BUT THIS WENT ON FOR YEARS.
BUT LET'S STOP HERE NOW THAT WE'VE ARRIVED.
NOW BE NICE AND QUIET, I DON'T WANT ANY TROUBLE.
OI! SISTERS, I CARRY A PRECIOUS CARGO.
I ASK FOR PERMISSION TO PASS.
JUST FROG CONVENIENCE
JUST FROG CONVENIENCE

GET OUT THE VEHICLE. SLOWLY.
VERY SLOWLY.
I'M ON A MISSION AND I CAN'T WASTE TIME.
YOUR MISSION IS NONE OF MY CONCERN.
I RECOGNIZE THE TWO OF YOU BUT NOT THE YOUNG ONES.
ONE IS CALLED MAISA, SISTER OF THE GREAT LAKES.
THE OTHER ONE IS AILIS, DAUGHTER OF OLIVIA OUR—
I KNOW WHO HER MOTHER IS, TRHICE-ACCURSED.
THE FAULT IS HERS TO BEAR!

ENOUGH!

ALRIGHT, CALM DOWN!
HIT THEM AND DON'T HOLD BACK!

LIGHT OF THE HEART!

EVERYBODY CALM DOWN, FOR FUCKS' SAKE!

NOW YOU'LL STOP ATTACKING US, OKAY?
BUT...
OKAY?

AND YOU LET HER GO, WE'RE ALL ON THE SAME SIDE.
DUNNO IF I WANT TO.
DENISE, PLEASE.

THANK YOU, MAISA. FINALLY SOMEONE THAT'S THINKING STRAIGHT.
I'M WAY TOO OLD AND TIRED FOR ALL THIS BULLSHIT. I JUST WANT TO REST.

YOU TWO AS WELL, GO FIND SOMEWHERE TO SLEEP. WE'RE LEAVING EARLY TOMORROW.
AND NOW, GOODNIGHT!

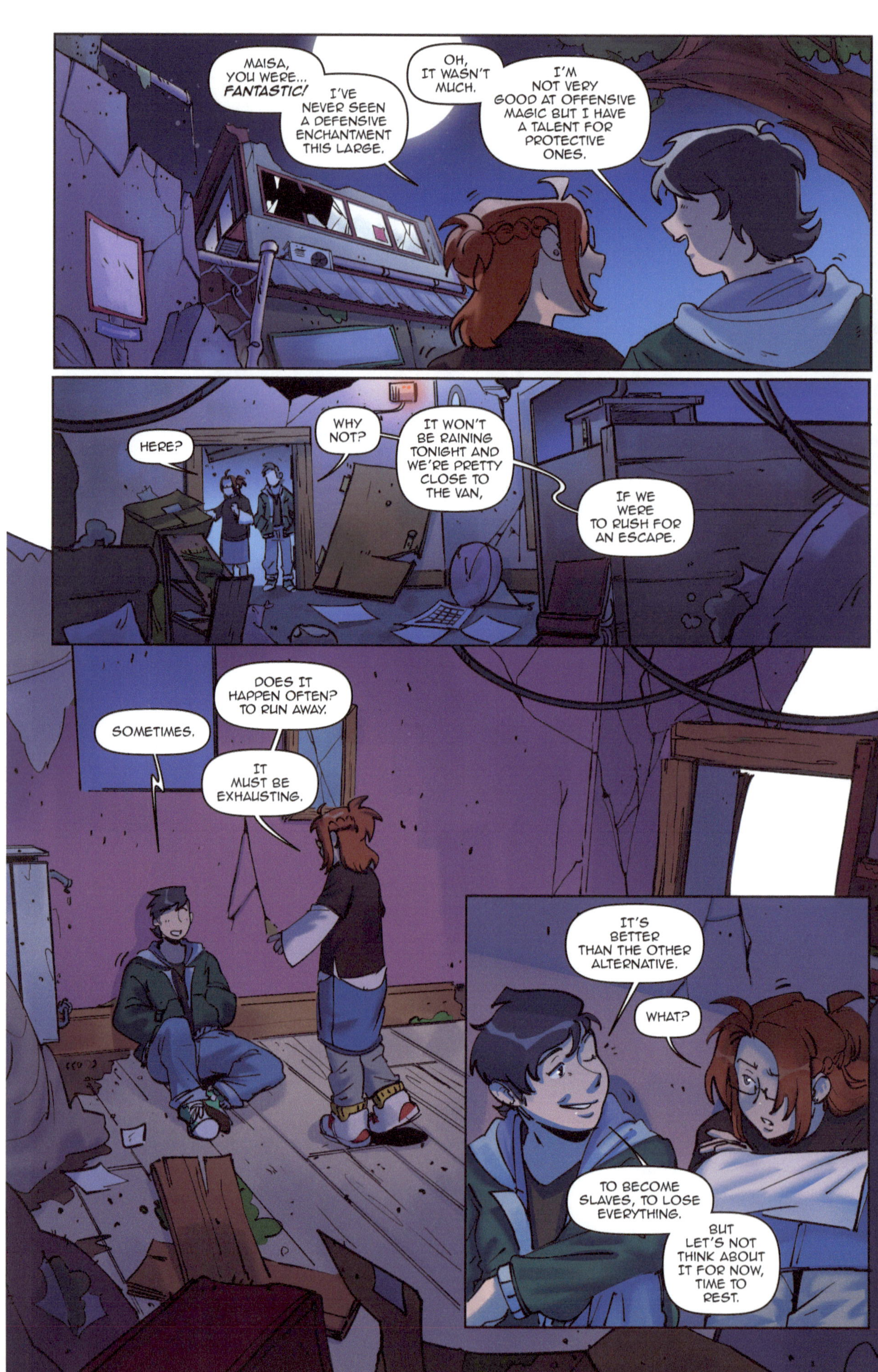

MAISA, YOU WERE... FANTASTIC! I'VE NEVER SEEN A DEFENSIVE ENCHANTMENT THIS LARGE.
OH, IT WASN'T MUCH.
I'M NOT VERY GOOD AT OFFENSIVE MAGIC BUT I HAVE A TALENT FOR PROTECTIVE ONES.
HERE?
WHY NOT?
IT WON'T BE RAINING TONIGHT AND WE'RE PRETTY CLOSE TO THE VAN,
IF WE WERE TO RUSH FOR AN ESCAPE.
DOES IT HAPPEN OFTEN? TO RUN AWAY.
SOMETIMES.
IT MUST BE EXHAUSTING.
IT'S BETTER THAN THE OTHER ALTERNATIVE.
WHAT?
TO BECOME SLAVES, TO LOSE EVERYTHING.
BUT LET'S NOT THINK ABOUT IT FOR NOW, TIME TO REST.

MY DAUGHTER ... DAUGHTER OF BLOOD...
MOM, WHERE ARE YOU? SO MANY THINGS ARE HAPPENING...
AND SO MANY THINGS WILL KEEP ON HAPPENING.
THE BLOOD NEEDS TO FLOW ONCE MORE...
MOM!
YOU'RE PAYING FOR FAULTS THAT AREN'T YOURS,
DAUGHTER OF BLOOD...
BUT YOU'LL PAY FOR THEM REGARDLESS.
MOM!
MOM!!

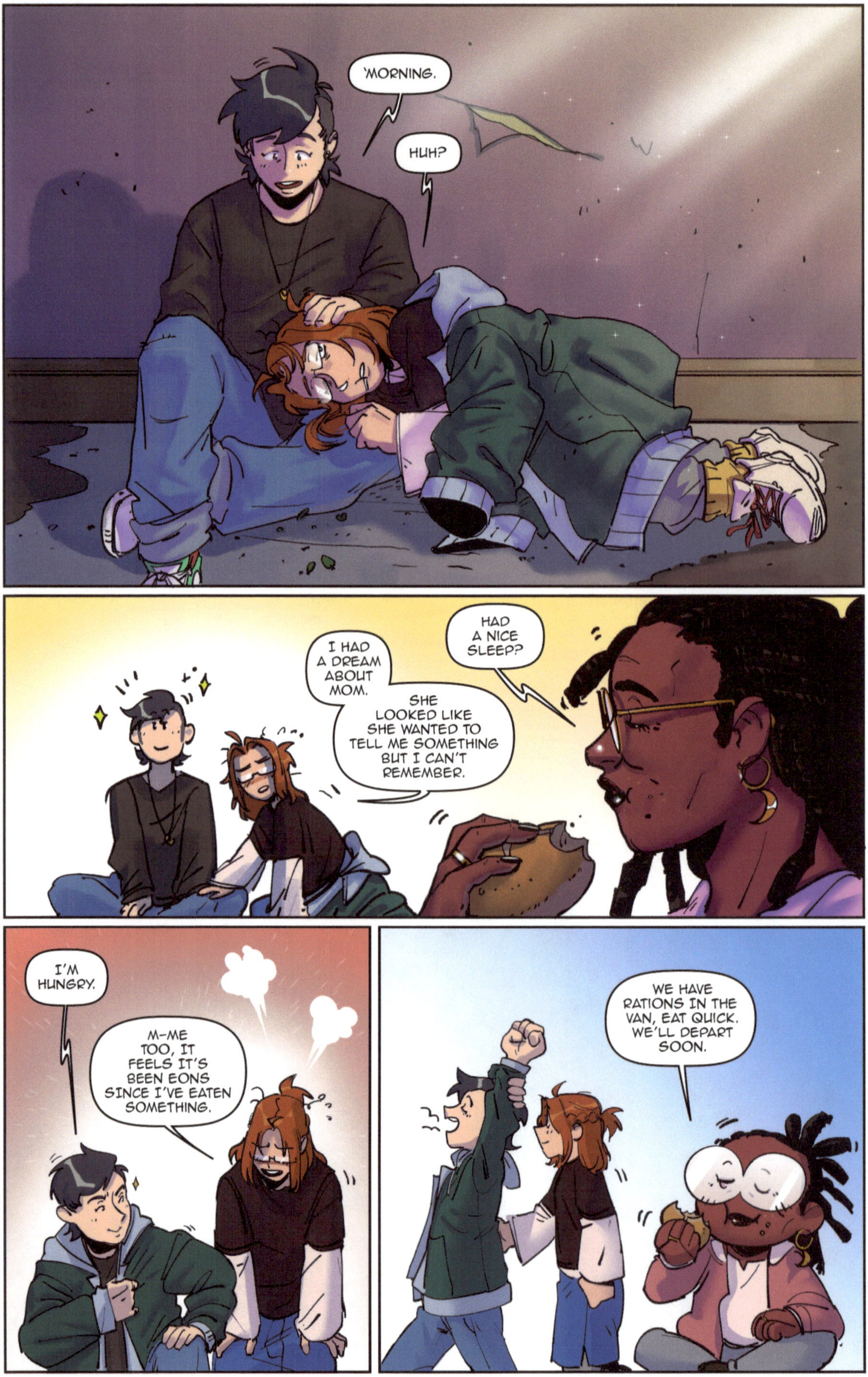

'MORNING.
HUH?
HAD A NICE SLEEP?
I HAD A DREAM ABOUT MOM.
SHE LOOKED LIKE SHE WANTED TO TELL ME SOMETHING BUT I CAN'T REMEMBER.

I'M HUNGRY.
M—ME TOO, IT FEELS IT'S BEEN EONS SINCE I'VE EATEN SOMETHING.

WE HAVE RATIONS IN THE VAN, EAT QUICK. WE'LL DEPART SOON.

I'D LOVE SOMETHING SWEET, MAYBE A CAKE!
SORRY TO DISAPPOINT BUT I THINK THERE'S ONLY LEFTOVER BREAD FROM THE OTHER DAY.
WE'RE UNDER ATTACK!
BANG

RUN, QUICK!
BANG
CRASH
BANG
HURRY!!
BANG
BANG
BANG
NO, NO...
NOOO!

MAISA...
MAISA!

AILIS!
AILIS, LISTEN TO ME... WE HAVE TO RUN AWAY FROM HERE.
MAISA... S-SHE GOT SHOT...
AND I COULDN'T DO ANYTHING...
I KNOW, DARLING. WE HAVE TO ESCAPE. NOW.

TURN ON THE ENGINE, WE'RE LEAVING IMMEDIATELY!

AILIS, YOU NEED TO MOVE OR MAISA WILL DIE HERE!

BLAM
BLAM
ZING
GET READY TO START THE VAN!
WHAT ABOUT THE OTHERS?!

THEY'LL MANAGE, WE HAVE A MISSION TO COMPLETE.
AILIS I NEED YOU HERE!
TLSC

VROOO
WE GOT COMPANY!
VROOOOO

THEY'RE ONTO US, AND MUCH FASTER!

IF THAT FOOL DOESN'T FLIP US FIRST. WE'LL BE BUSY FIGHTING THEM BACK.
YOU HAVE TO TAKE CARE OF MAISA.

AILIS!!
I NEED YOU, MAISA NEEDS YOU!!

Y-YES.
RIGHT.

DON'T WORRY, DENISE. I'LL TAKE CARE OF HER.
ARE WE IN DANGER?
DANGER?
OF COURSE, WE'RE ABOUT TO DIE.
ISN'T THAT EXCITING?

WHERE THE HELL IS IT?
DID SOMEBODY THROW IT AWAY?!

AH, HOW MUCH I'VE MISSED YOU.
LET'S HAVE SOME FUN NOW!

CAREFUL NOT TO MAKE ME FALL OFF LIKE LAST TIME!
BLAM
BLAM
BLAM
SKREEEE

VROOOOOO
WE HAVE GUESTS.
KA
BLAM
HAHAHA!!
PSHH

LEAVE THE ROAD, LET'S MAKE IT HARDER FOR THEM TO CHASE US!

WITH THIS PIECE OF JUNK?! ARE YOU OUT OF YOUR MIND?!

YES, DO IT!

SKREEE
VROOOOO

VRRRRR

NOW IT'S MY TURN!

BLAM
SHIT!
CRASH
BLAM
AGH!
ZING
THUD

TURN!!
THEY'RE GONNA SHOOT US WITH A BAZOOKA!!!

FSHHHHHHH
VRRRROOOO
FSHHHH

LIGHT OF THE SUN...
LIGHT OF MY BLOOD!

WHOOOSH
VROOOOOOOOOO
KABLAM
BOOM
THANK GOD IT WORKED, I NEVER TRIED DOING SOMETHING LIKE THA--
AILIS, AILIS!!!

SHE'S AWAKE!

WHAT HAPPENED?! WHERE ARE WE?
MAISA?

YOU SAVED US.
WE'RE SOMEWHERE NEAR SANTA FE.
MAISA IS RESTING.
DID THAT ANSWER TO ALL OF YOUR QUESTIONS?

HOW IS SHE?
SHE'S STABLE FOR NOW,
BUT NONE OF US IS GOOD ENOUGH WITH HEALING MAGIC.
IS THERE ANYONE WHO CAN HELP?
IT'S NOT THAT SIMPLE.
SO THERE IS SOMEONE??
NO.
THERE IS A WITCH IN SANTA FE...
IF YOU CAN SUGGEST SOMEONE DIFFERENT THEN...
THIS IS WRONG, IT'S NOT FAIR.
THEN NAME SOMEONE ELSE WHO CAN SAVE MAISA'S LIFE AND WE'RE GOING IMMEDIATELY.
I KNOW THERE'S NO ONE ELSE, BUT DO AS YOU PLEASE, LIKE YOU ALWAYS DO!

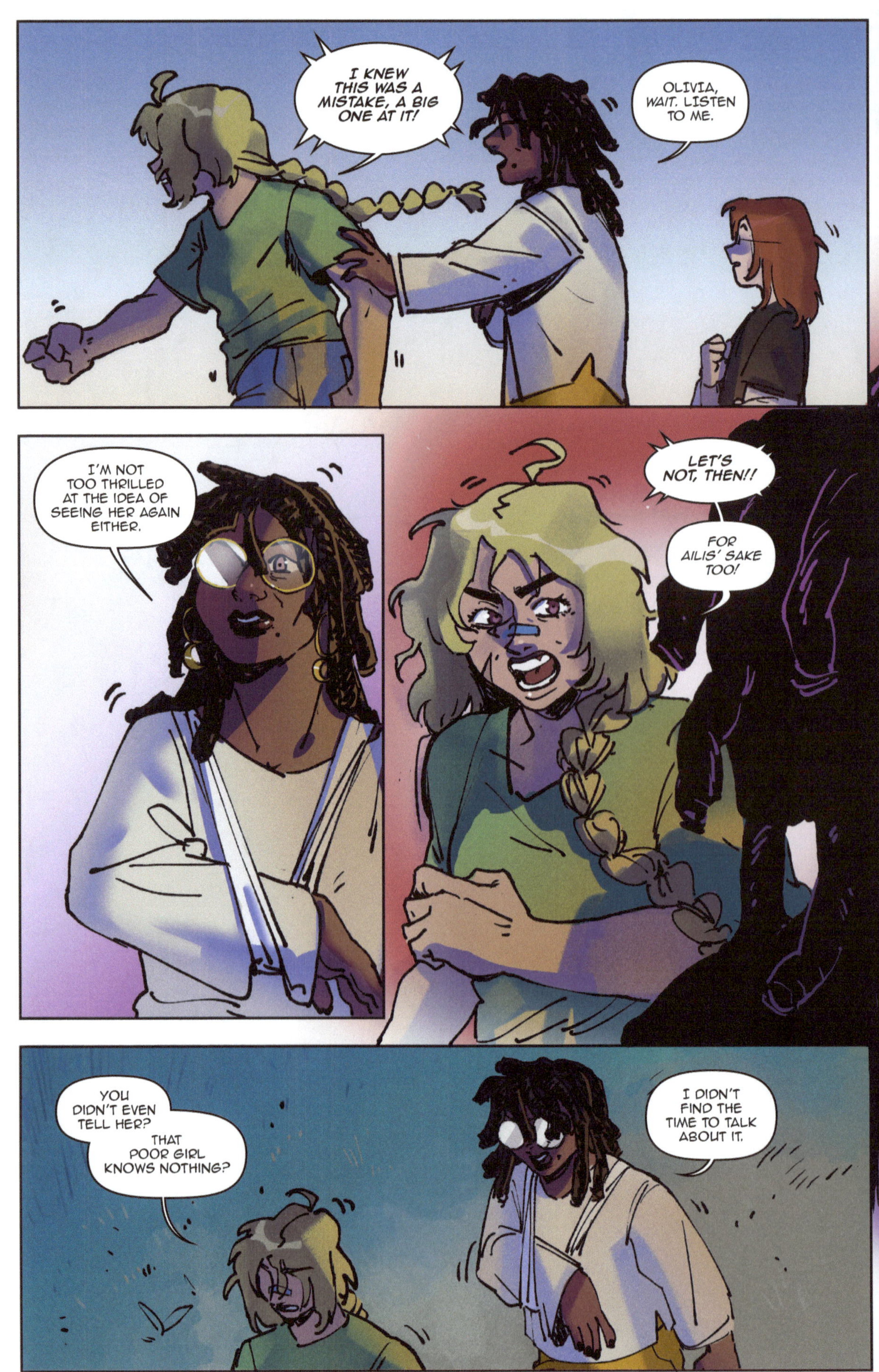

I KNEW THIS WAS A MISTAKE, A BIG ONE AT IT!
OLIVIA, WAIT. LISTEN TO ME.
I'M NOT TOO THRILLED AT THE IDEA OF SEEING HER AGAIN EITHER.
LET'S NOT, THEN!!
FOR AILIS' SAKE TOO!
YOU DIDN'T EVEN TELL HER? THAT POOR GIRL KNOWS NOTHING?
I DIDN'T FIND THE TIME TO TALK ABOUT IT.

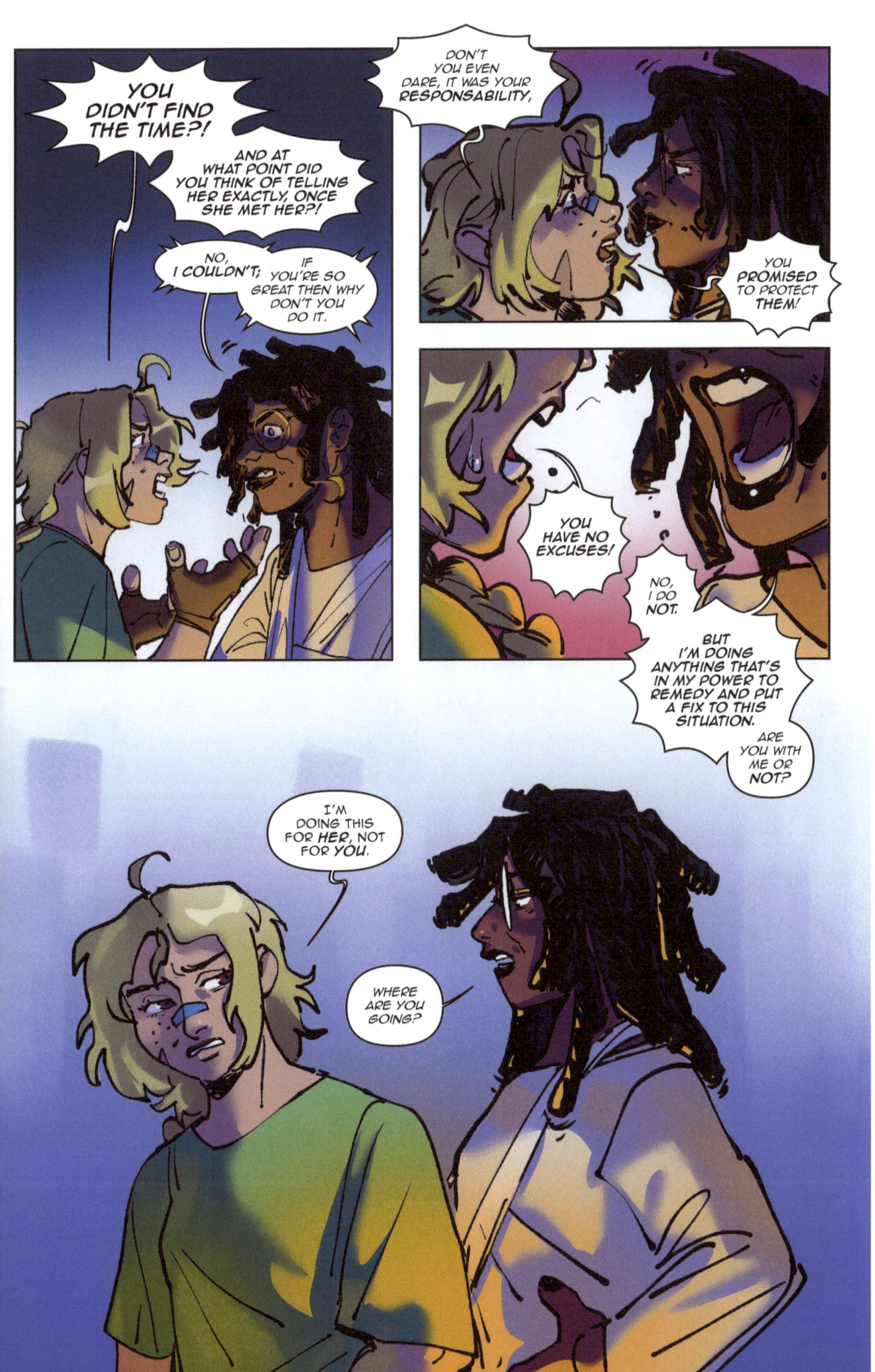

YOU DIDN'T FIND THE TIME?!
AND AT WHAT POINT DID YOU THINK OF TELLING HER EXACTLY, ONCE SHE MET HER?!
NO, I COULDN'T;
IF YOU'RE SO GREAT THEN WHY DON'T YOU DO IT.
DON'T YOU EVEN DARE, IT WAS YOUR RESPONSABILITY,
YOU PROMISED TO PROTECT THEM!
YOU HAVE NO EXCUSES!
NO, I DO NOT.
BUT I'M DOING ANYTHING THAT'S IN MY POWER TO REMEDY AND PUT A FIX TO THIS SITUATION.
ARE YOU WITH ME OR NOT?
I'M DOING THIS FOR HER, NOT FOR YOU.
WHERE ARE YOU GOING?

WHERE? TO SANTA FE, BUT I'M DONE WITH YOU.
AFTER THIS DUTY I DON'T WANT TO SEE YOU EVER AGAIN.
EVER. AGAIN.

WE HAVE TO DEPART IMMEDIATELY.
AILIS, HELP ME WITH MAISA.
NO, THERE'S THINGS NOT EVEN MAGIC CAN MEND.
IS EVERYTHING ALRIGHT BETWEEN YOU TWO?

WHAT EVEN IS GOING ON? I HAD A NORMAL LIFE TILL A FEW DAYS AGO.

LET'S TRY TO LEAVE AS SOON AS WE CAN.
I'LL TRY TO EXPLAIN AS MUCH AS I CAN WHILE WE'RE ON OUR WAY.

NOW, DENISE.

I'M EXHAUSTED, I'LL DO IT ONCE WE GET THERE.

DO IT NOW OR I'M STOPPING THE VAN.

FINE.
AILIS, YOU ASKED ME ABOUT WHAT HAD HAPPENED.
YEAH...
FIRST AND FOREMOST, YOU HAVE NO FAULTS IN THIS.
A FEW FORCES THAT WERE BORN MANY YEARS AGO ARE STARTING TO MAKE THEIR MOVE.
WHAT DOES IT MEAN?
I'VE KNOWN YOUR MOTHER EVER SINCE WE WERE JUST TWO APPRENTICES,
WE WANTED TO CHANGE THE WORLD AND WE WERE GIVEN THE CHANCE TO DO SO.
WE THOUGHT IT WAS A SMART CHOICE BACK THEN.
WE NEEDED STRONGER WAYS, WE'VE NEVER SEEN A WITCH LIKE HER.
BUT IN ORDER TO DO THAT, WE NEEDED TO UNITE TWO DIFFERENT KINDS OF MAGIC.
WE NEEDED IMBUE OUR MAGIC WITH DARKNESS...

OUR AGENTS FAILED THE MISSION, AND WE'VE LOST TRACK OF THE FUGITIVES.
DON'T WORRY, THEY WILL BRING MY DAUGHTER TO ME.